My Daddy

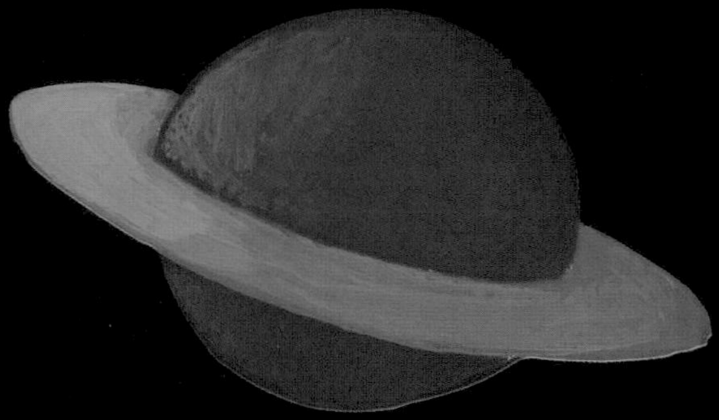

My

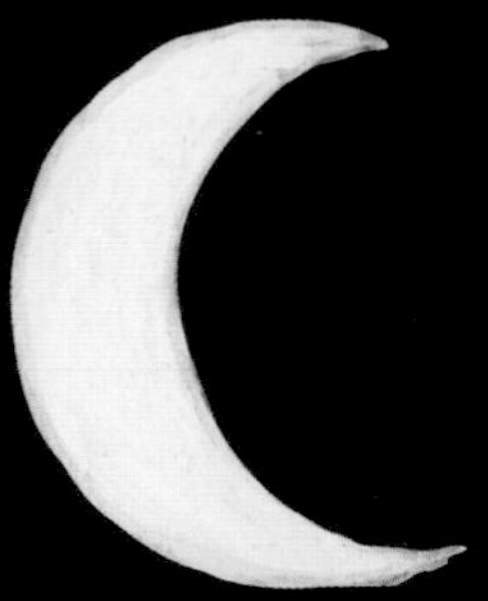

To Dad, the best grandpa in the world C.J.

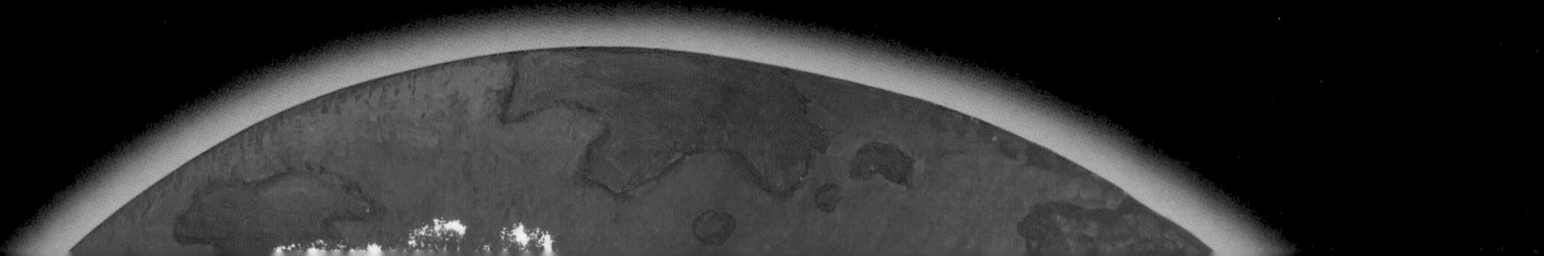

Daddy

CURTIS JOBLING

Collins

An imprint of HarperCollinsPublishers

Sophie and Sue and Molly (that's me),
we like to go to the park.
We swing and we talk
and we talk and we swing.

But sometimes I just listen.

"My daddy is the best daddy
in the whole world," says Sophie.
"He's so strong, he can pick me up
with one hand."

"My daddy's even better," says Sue.
"He's so strong . . .

. . . he always wins the tug of war, all by himself."

"But **my daddy**," says Sophie, "is the cleverest daddy in the whole world."

"But my daddy's even cleverer," says Sue. "He always wins prizes."

"But my daddy," says Sophie, "wins...

"My daddy," says Sue, "is the bravest daddy in the whole world.

He isn't scared of bugs or slugs
or big fat hairy spiders."

"But **my daddy**, he's even braver,"
says **Sophie**.

"Giant snakes and giant spiders.
They're all afraid of HIM.
He tames them with his fierce glare
and flarey nostrils!"

He loves wrestling with sharks and octopuses."

"My daddy got bored with taming sharks," says Sophie.

"Now he tames DINOSAURS . . ."

"My daddy's
the KING—"

"My daddy's an
ACTION HERO..."

"My daddy's a SUPER HERO!"

"My daddy's a SUPER DOOPER HERO!!"

"My daddy's FATHER CHRISTMAS!!!"

"Oh, yeah?"
says Sophie.

"What does YOUR daddy do?"
they ask.

And I tell them...

"Ooh, you big fat fibber!" says Sophie.
"Nobody likes a show-off!" says Sue.

"Did I ever tell you about my mummy?"

First published in Great Britain in 2004 by HarperCollins Children's Books. 10 9 8 7 6 5 4 3 2 1 ISBN: 0 00 712255 1 HarperCollins Children's Books is a division of HarperCollins Publishers Ltd, 77-85 Fulham Palace Road, Hammersmith, London W6 8JB. Text and illustrations copyright © Curtis Jobling 2004 All rights reserved. Printed and bound in China by Imago

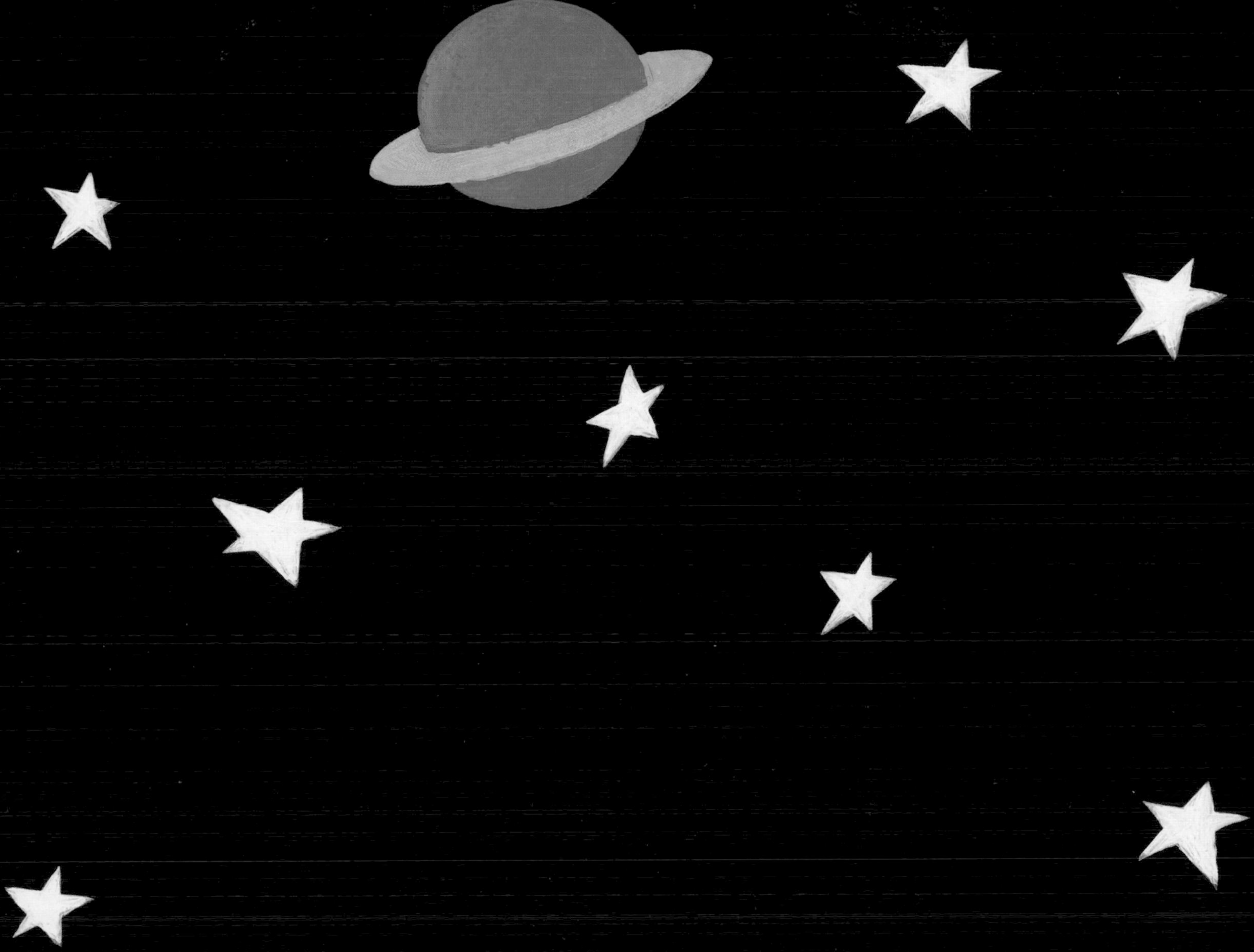

Every child deserves the best...

0-00-664627-1

0-00-712211-X

0-00-710794-3

0-00-717236-2

0-00-664775-8

0-00-710624-6

0-00-664777-4

0-00-714969-7

0-00-716031-3

0-00-664728-6

Collins

An imprint of HarperCollinsPublishers